S0-AWG-847

A Pukeko in a Ponga Tree

A Pukeko in a Ponga

Adapted by Kingi M. Ihaka
Illustrated by Dick Frizzell

Tree (The Twelve Days of Christmas)

On the first day of Christmas
my true love gave to me
a pukeko in a ponga tree

On the second day of Christmas
my true love gave to me
two kumara
and a pukeko in a ponga tree

On the third day of Christmas
my true love gave to me
three flax kits
two kumara
and a pukeko in a ponga tree

On the fourth day of Christmas
my true love gave to me
four huhu grubs
three flax kits
two kumara
and a pukeko in a ponga tree

On the fifth day of Christmas
my true love gave to me
five big fat pigs
four huhu grubs
three flax kits
two kumara
and a pukeko in a ponga tree

On the sixth day of Christmas
my true love gave to me
six poi a twirling
five big fat pigs
four huhu grubs
three flax kits
two kumara
and a pukeko in a ponga tree

On the seventh day of Christmas
my true love gave to me
seven eels a swimming
six poi a twirling
five big fat pigs
four huhu grubs
three flax kits
two kumara
and a pukeko in a ponga tree

On the eighth day of Christmas
my true love gave to me
eight plants of puha
seven eels a swimming
six poi a twirling
five big fat pigs
four huhu grubs
three flax kits
two kumara
and a pukeko in a ponga tree

On the ninth day of Christmas
my true love gave to me
nine sacks of pipi
eight plants of puha
seven eels a swimming
six poi a twirling
five big fat pigs
four huhu grubs
three flax kits
two kumara
and a pukeko in a ponga tree

On the tenth day of Christmas
my true love gave to me
ten juicy fish heads
nine sacks of pipi
eight plants of puha
seven eels a swimming
six poi a twirling
five big fat pigs
four huhu grubs
three flax kits
two kumara
and a pukeko in a ponga tree

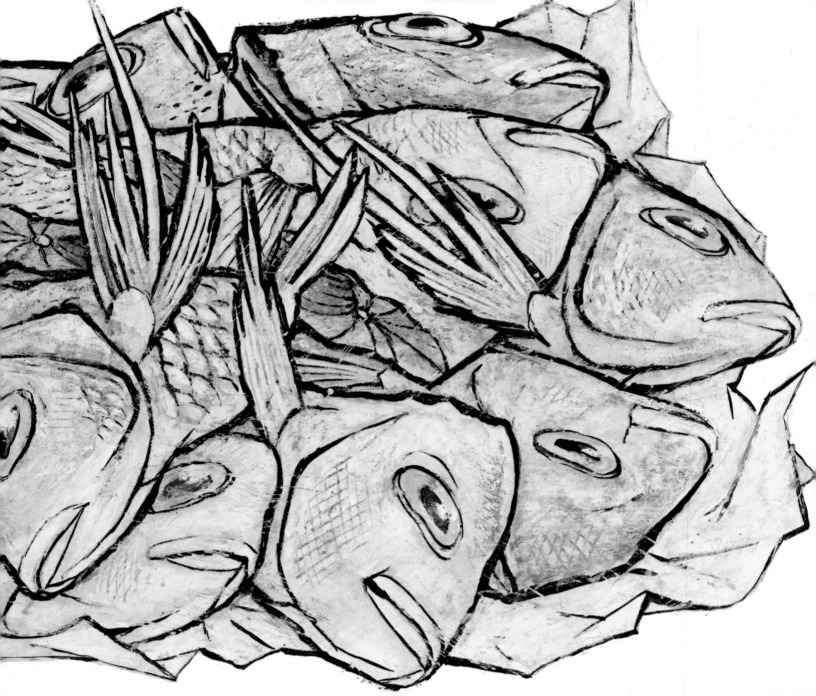

On the eleventh day of Christmas
my true love gave to me
eleven haka lessons
ten juicy fish heads
nine sacks of pipi
eight plants of puha
seven eels a swimming
six poi a twirling
five big fat pigs
four huhu grubs
three flax kits
two kumara
and a pukeko in a ponga tree

On the twelfth day of Christmas
my true love gave to me
twelve piupiu swinging
eleven haka lessons
ten juicy fish heads
nine sacks of pipi
eight plants of puha
seven eels a swimming
six poi a twirling
five big fat pigs
four huhu grubs
three flax kits
two kumara
and a pukeko in a ponga tree

Puffin Books
Published by the Penguin Group
Penguin Group (NZ), 67 Apollo Drive, Rosedale,
North Shore 0632, New Zealand (a division of Pearson New Zealand Ltd)

Penguin Books Ltd, Registered Offices: 80 Strand, London, WC2R 0RL, England

First published in New Zealand 1981 by Heinemann Reed
Published 1991 by Little Mammoth New Zealand (an imprint of Reed Publishing (NZ) Ltd)
Reprinted 1993, 1994, 1995, 1996, 1998, 1999, 2000, 2001, 2003, 2004, 2006, 2007

First published in Puffin Books, 2008
This edition published in Puffin Books, 2011
10 9 8 7 6 5 4 3 2 1

Copyright © Kingi M. Ihaka and Dick Frizzell, 1981

The authors assert their moral rights. All Rights reserved.

Printed in China through Bookbuilders, Hong Kong

ISBN: 9 78 0 14350505 1